Fairly Fairy Tales

By Esmé Raji Codell

Illustrated by Elisa Chavarri

Aladdin

New York   London   Toronto   Sydney

For Russell, definitely

—E.R.C.

For Matthew, my love

—E.C.

ALADDIN

An imprint of Simon & Schuster Children's Publishing Division

1230 Avenue of the Americas, New York, NY 10020

First Aladdin hardcover edition January 2011

For information about special discounts for bulk purchases, please contact Simon & Schuster Special Sales at 1-866-506-1949 or business@simonandschuster.com.

The Simon & Schuster Speakers Bureau can bring authors to your live event. For more information or to book an event contact the Simon & Schuster Speakers Bureau at 1-866-248-3049 or visit our website at www.simonspeakers.com.

Designed by Lisa Vega

The text of this book was set in Hawaiian Aloha BTN and Carrotflower.

The illustrations for this book were digitally rendered.

Manufactured in China 1215 SCP

10 9 8 7 6 5 4

Library of Congress Cataloging-in-Publication Data

Codell, Esmé Raji, 1968-

Fairly fairy tales / by Esmé Raji Codell.—1st Aladdin hardcover ed.

p. cm.

Summary: Offers a different look at some classic stories, as a parent and child read before bedtime.

ISBN 978-1-4169-9086-4 (hardcover)

[1. Fairy tales—Fiction. 2. Books and reading—Fiction.

3. Humorous stories.] I. Title.

PZ7.C649Fai 2011   [E]—dc22   2009016475

Once upon
a time . . .

Kiss?

Yes.

Water?

Yes.

Bedtime?

NOOOOO!

Sticks?
Yes.

Straw?
Yes.

Bricks?

Yes.

Solar
panels?

NOOOOO!

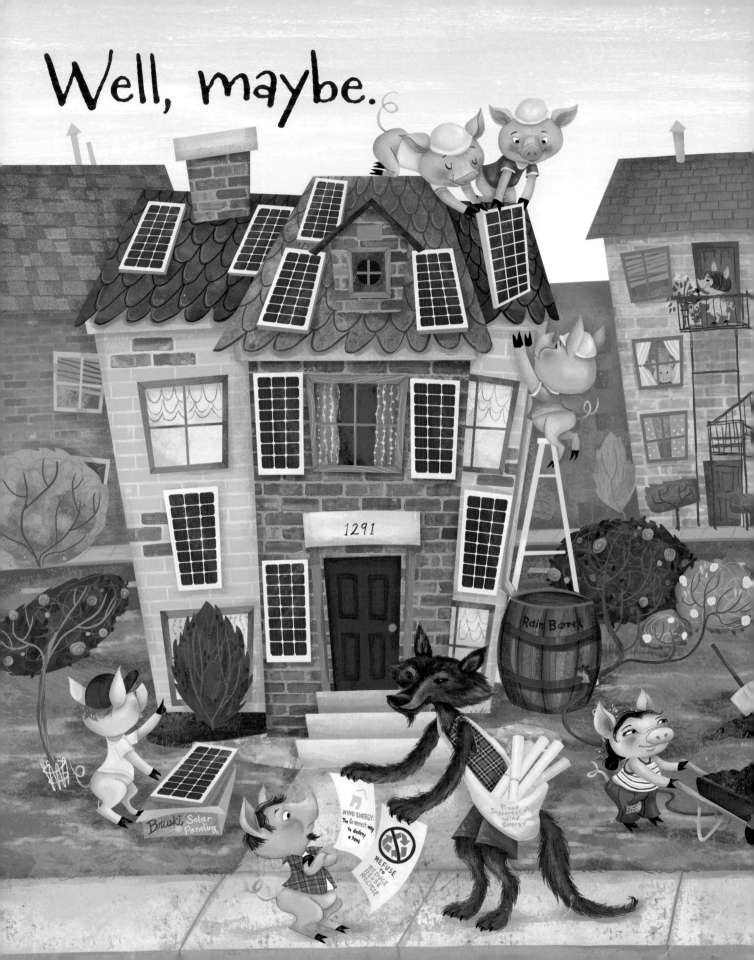

Red hood?
Yes.

Wolf?
Yes.

Grandma?
Yes.

Shampoo?

NOOOOO!

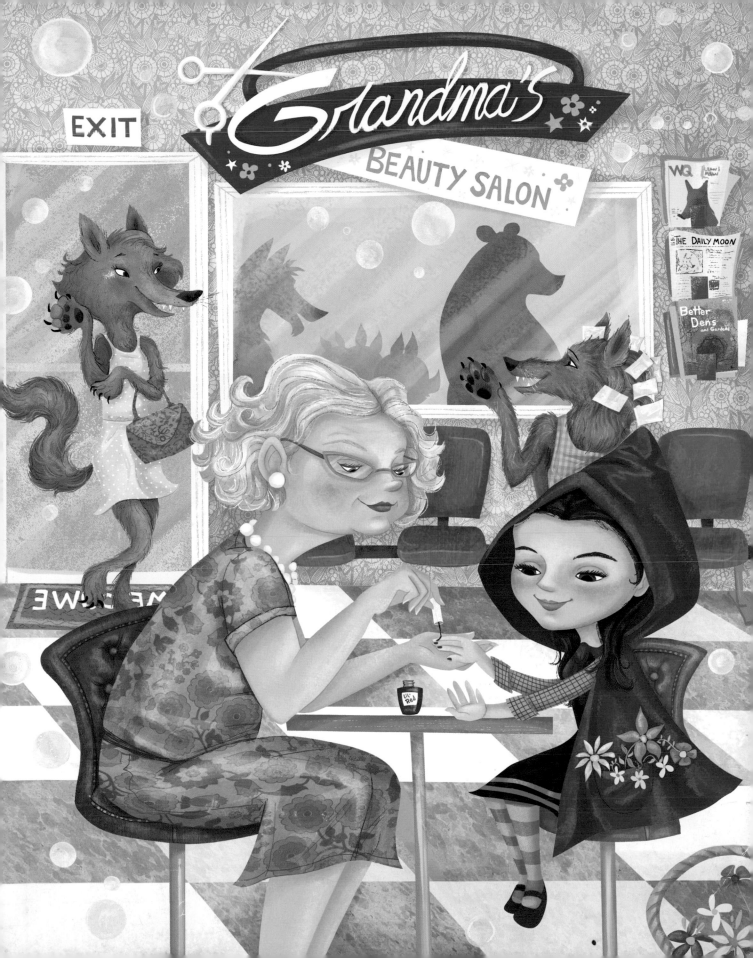

Cow? Yes.

Beanstalk? Yes.

Giant? Yes.

Spaghetti?

NOOOOO!

Well, maybe.

Fairy godmother? Yes.

Pumpkin coach? Yes.

Bread crumbs?

Yes.

Gingerbread?

Yes.

Witch?
Yes.

Piñata?
NOOOOO!

Well, maybe.

Porridge?
Yes.

Chair?
Yes.

Bed?
Yes.

Television?
NOOOOO!

Well, maybe.

Kiss?
Yes.

Water?
Yes.

Bedtime?

Well, maybe.